The big street with its cafés and shops and people was behind them now. They walked slowly.

It was quiet. Away from the cars and the noise, Kim was excited. She held on to Dave's hand.

They were in a narrow street of tall houses and small shops. They heard a radio through an open window. A woman singing. Kim stopped and listened, but she did not understand the words. Her Spanish was good, but not very good!

It was the fourth day of their stay in Barcelona.

Kim and Dave were seventeen. They had the same Spanish teacher at school in Liverpool, a big town in England. 'Do you want to talk Spanish?' their teacher said. 'Well, go to Spain!'

There were eight of them from the same school on this holiday. They went to school every morning and talked Spanish. Then, in the afternoons, they usually went out by bus and saw something in Barcelona – important buildings, famous pictures, old photographs. Something new every day.

Today, Kim and Dave were not with their school friends. Dave did not want to go by bus. He wanted to look round the old town. Not the famous buildings. Not the big shopping streets with the banks and cafés and bookshops. He was interested in the little streets behind the old market. The 'dangerous' old town, people said. But Dave was not frightened. 'There are "dangerous" streets in Liverpool, too,' he said.

You can't see a town or its people only from a bus.

It will be exciting.

They did not try to remember the names of the streets. They did not have a street plan. At every corner they stopped and looked. Then they came to an interesting little street. It was very narrow. Very old, they thought. Dave took a photograph.

Kim looked up. The houses were very tall. The windows up there were in the sun. But down in the street it was dark.

They came to a little open place with two or three trees and sat down. It was quiet.

Suddenly, there was a noise in one of the houses. A door opened and a man in a black shirt and jeans ran out. He stood at the open door and looked back into the house. Then he ran across the street.

'Is he coming over here?' Kim asked. There was something frightening about the man.

Dave did not answer. The man ran to the corner and looked around. Then he ran away.

There were shouts from the house. A second man ran out into the street. He had long hair and dark glasses. He stood in the road and looked round.

'Perhaps he's looking for that man in the black shirt,' said Dave. 'And look! He's got a gun!'

Kim looked. Dave was right! The long-haired man ran across the street and went round the corner.

'Let's get away from here,' Kim said. 'I don't like this.'

But Dave was excited. 'Let's go and have a look in that rubbish bin,' he said.

There was a brown box in the bin. Dave took it out and opened it. A small white bag fell out.

'Drugs!' he said. 'We'll take this to the police.'

Kim took the little white bag and held it in her hand. She was suddenly very frightened. She looked round. Behind them there was a man, there under the trees. Watching them.

The man moved. Kim looked at the bag in her hand. Suddenly she knew.

'Dave, that man – he's back! He's here!' she said.

The man was very near them now. He was not very tall, with a thin, white face and dark, dangerous eyes.

'Give it to me,' he said in Spanish. His frightening eyes moved quickly from Kim to Dave and back to Kim.

Kim opened her mouth but the words did not come out. 'Oh, Dave,' she thought, '*do* something!' But Dave did not move.

Then she saw the knife in the man's hand. She started to run. She ran into a small street on the left.

She ran down two or three narrow streets. But she did not see any people. She heard him behind her.

I'll soon find some people. Then he won't catch me.

'Quick,' she thought. 'I can't stop.'

But all the streets were the same. Where was she now? Suddenly, she came round a corner and her legs went cold. The street did not go through – it stopped. There were some cars and a big old building. An old cinema, perhaps. But there was no road through.

Kim looked back. The man stood at the corner and waited. He started to walk slowly down the street.

Kim looked round. There was a door in the building.
She ran to it. It opened! She went in and shut the door
behind her.

Noise. People. Women. Talking, shouting, moving
their arms. The market! She was in the market in the
old town, near the big shopping street. That door was a
back door to the market and the big street was very
near.

She started to walk through the market. She was in a slow-moving river of people with heavy shopping bags. She moved with the river. Every time one person stopped and looked at some fruit or fish, all of them stopped. Kim wanted to go quickly, but it was not easy. All these women with bags of food for the family!

Then, in the sea of faces, Kim saw those same dark eyes again. Watching her. He was here in the market!

Kim started to run. There were shopping bags under her feet. She fell and got up again. People shouted at her. One woman tried to catch hold of her, but Kim did not stop.

Then she looked back. The man was not behind her now. Perhaps she was wrong. Those eyes – perhaps it was not the same man. She saw the big street now. She saw the sun and the trees.

Suddenly, a hand came down on her arm and held on to her.

'Are you Kim Steele?' the woman asked. She was tall, about thirty. She had a friendly look.

Kim did not understand. 'Yes,' she started to say, 'but how do you . . . ?'

Then, in the woman's hand, she saw a photo and, in Spanish, the word POLICE.

The policewoman smiled. 'Your friend Dave found us. He's in the car. Come with me.'

Kim sat in the car with Dave. There was a man with
Ana. He had long hair and dark glasses. Now Kim
understood: he was a policeman, too.

She gave Ana the little white bag and asked about
the man with the knife. 'He sells drugs, is that it?'

'That's right,' Ana said. She looked at the long-haired
man. 'Nacho here nearly caught him in his house. You
saw that. Vidal – that's his name – was lucky. He got
away. But we want him, and you can do something for
us.'

Nacho smiled.

'Y-y-yes,' Kim said slowly, 'but . . .'

Vidal knows you now, Kim. And he wants his drugs. Listen. This is my plan.

You go back to that place near Vidal's house. Vidal will be there and he'll see you. We'll be there, too, but Vidal won't see us. He'll think, 'She's looking for her friend.'

I can't do it.

Don't be frightened. Vidal won't get near you — we'll stop him, but he'll try . . .

And then we'll catch him!

17

Kim said 'yes' and Nacho talked on the car radio. Then they drove round behind the market. Kim got out and shut the car door. She walked to the corner, then she looked back. Ana smiled at her. Dave's face was very white.

Kim was frightened. These things were exciting in the cinema, but this was not a game. Ana and Nacho were there – she knew that. But this Vidal was clever. Perhaps he knew about their little plan. And he was dangerous.

She was back in the same street now. There was the house. The door was shut. And there was the rubbish bin. Two or three people came down the street. Kim walked slowly across the road. She looked round, then up at the windows of the houses. She waited.

He's here. He's watching me. I can feel it.

Then she saw him. The black shirt, the thin face, those eyes – it was Vidal. He was very near her.

Kim looked across the street. She was ready to run, then she heard Vidal. He said something, the same thing again and again.

'What's he saying?' Kim thought. 'Is he talking to me?'

She looked at him. He did not move. Only his mouth moved. This time she understood the words.

'Give it to me or you're dead,' he said.

A car drove round the corner very quickly and stopped. Ana and Nacho jumped out. They held guns. Ana shouted.

Police, don't move! We've got guns.

Vidal suddenly jumped at Kim and caught her. Kim tried to hit him, to get away, but he held on to her hair. He was thin, but strong. Then she saw the knife.

'You'll be sorry, Vidal!' Nacho shouted. 'You can't get out of here. Think, man!'

Throw the knife down and take your hands from the girl!

But Vidal held on to Kim. He shouted to the police. 'Get back in the car, or I'll do it!'

He held the knife near Kim's face. She shut her eyes. Time moved very slowly. She saw a face at the window of one of the houses across the road.

Ana and Nacho moved back to the car. Their guns were ready, but Vidal stood behind Kim.

Suddenly, there were excited shouts from behind the police car. It was Dave. He ran across the street.

'What's he doing?' Kim thought. 'Does he want to see me dead?'

Ana tried to stop him. 'Come back! This man is dangerous!' she shouted.

Dave ran to the rubbish bin. He stopped, took the bin in his hands and held it up over his head. Then he threw it.

The rubbish bin went over Kim's head and hit Vidal. Rubbish fell round his feet. He fell. Kim quickly took the knife from his hand and threw it away.

There were excited shouts. Kim looked up. It was Ana and Nacho.

'He's all yours, now,' said Dave.

Nacho held Vidal's hands behind his back and took him away. Kim fell into Ana's arms.

Later, they drove back to the hotel in a police car. Kim looked at Dave.

Don't say it! I know. It was dangerous. But I saw the bin and I thought, well, you know . . . I wanted to *do* something. I see these things in the cinema. There's always a strong man. Today, I was the strong man.

Yes, and I was nearly the dead girlfriend. You see a lot of them in the cinema, too!

ACTIVITIES

Before you read

1 Look at the pictures on pages 1–10. What are the people doing? Where are they? What are they going to do?
2 Look at the Word List at the back of the book.
    a What are the words in your language?
    b Can you see any of these things in the pictures?

While you read

3 Read pages 1–4. Which word in *italics* is right?
    a Kim and Dave are *Spanish / English*.
    b They live in *England / Spain*.
    c They are on holiday in *Liverpool / Barcelona*.
4 Are these sentences right (✓) or wrong (✗)?
    a Today Kim and Dave want to do some shopping.   .....
    b The old town is dangerous.   .....
    c Dave is frightened.   .....
5 Read pages 5–14. What comes first? And after that? Write the numbers 1–6.
    a ..... Kim and Dave find some drugs in the rubbish bin.
    b ..... Kim goes into the old market.
    c ..... Kim and Dave see a man in a black shirt.
    d ..... Kim talks to a policewoman.
    e ..... Kim starts to run through the old town.
    f ..... The man comes back and he has a knife.
    g ..... The man puts something in a rubbish bin.
6 Read pages 14–19. Finish the sentences on the left with words on the right.
    a The man with long hair .....   **f** wants to catch Vidal.
    b Ana .....   **g** want to use Kim.
    c The police .....   **h** wants the bag of drugs.
    d Dave .....   **i** stays in the police car.
    e Vidal .....   **j** is a policeman.

7 Read pages 20–26. Who says these things? Write *Kim*, *Vidal*, *Ana*, *Dave* or *Nacho*.

   a 'Give it to me or you're dead'.   .....

   b 'We've got guns.'   .....

   c 'This man is dangerous.'   .....

   d 'I wanted to *do* something.'   .....

   e 'You can't see a town only from a bus.'   .....

After you read

  8 Why are these things important in the story?

   a a white bag   **b** dark eyes   **c** a rubbish bin   **d** a bus

  9 Talk about the people in the story. (How old are they? Where are they from? What do they do? …)

Writing

10 Here are some sentences about Nacho.

Nacho is Spanish. He is tall and he has long, dark hair. He is about 30 years old. He is a policeman. He likes catching bad people.

Now write about Kim, Dave, Ana and Vidal.

11 Work with a friend. You are Kim and a policeman. Write questions and answers. Start with this question:

Policeman: *Where did you find the drugs?*

12 You are on holiday with your school friends in a famous town. Write a letter to your family.

13 What do you know about Barcelona? Read or ask people about it, and then write six sentences about Barcelona.

WORD LIST *with example sentences*

bin (n) We don't want that old food. Put it in the *bin*.

corner (n) The shop is on the *corner* of New Street and Oxford Street.

dangerous (adj) Don't go near the animals; they are *dangerous*.

drug (n) The police stopped her. Now she's at the police station because she had *drugs* in her bag.

excited (adj) The children are *excited* about the holiday. It's very *exciting* for them.

fell (v) He *fell* off his bicycle yesterday.

frightened (adj) Some children are *frightened* of dark rooms. Dark rooms can be *frightening*.

gun (n) Get down! That man's got a *gun*!

hold (v) She *held* his hand, and they walked across the road.

market (n) You can buy fruit in the shop or in the *market*.

ran (v) The policeman said 'Stop!' but the man *ran* away.

round (prep, adv) She looked *round* and saw a man behind her. This is an interesting town. Do you want to look *round* it?

rubbish (n) Do you want this old newspaper, or is it *rubbish*?

saw (v) I didn't see him, but my friend *saw* him.

sell (v) He buys and *sells* cars; that's his job.

shout (v, n) The teacher was very angry; he *shouted* at the boy.

something (pron) There's *something* on the floor. What is it?

thought (v) He didn't *think* about people; he only *thought* about money.

through (prep, adv) Did he come in *through* the door or the window?

took (v) I didn't take much money with me, but he *took* a lot.

The Adventures of Tom Sawyer
Mark Twain

Tom Sawyer loves adventures. He has them at home, at school,
and with his friends – Huck Finn, Joe Harper, and Becky Thatcher.
Tom has one adventure in a graveyard, one in an old house,
one in a cave. Who does he see in those places – and why is he
afraid?

Twenty Thousand Leagues under the Sea
Jules Verne

This is the story of Captain Nemo and his submarine, the *Nautilus*.
One day, Nemo finds three men in the sea. For months the men
live on the *Nautilus*. They find a town on the sea floor, beautiful
coasts and a lot of gold. But they want to go home. Can they
escape from Nemo's submarine?.

Rip Van Winkle and The Legend of Sleepy Hollow
Washington Irving

Rip Van Winkle walks into the mountains one day and meets some
strange old men. He comes home twenty years later. One dark
night, Ichabod Crane is riding home and sees a man on a black
horse behind him. The man has no head. Are there ghosts in these
stories? What do you think?

*There are hundreds of Penguin Readers to choose from – world classics,
film adaptations, modern-day crime and adventure, short stories,
biographies, American classics, non-fiction, plays ...*

For a complete list of all Penguin Readers titles, please contact your local
Pearson Longman office or visit our website.

www.penguinreaders.com

Pearson Education Limited
Edinburgh Gate, Harlow,
Essex CM20 2JE, England
and Associated Companies throughout the world.

ISBN: 978-1-4058-6970-6

First published by Penguin Books Ltd 1996
Published by Addison Wesley Longman Ltd and Penguin Books Ltd 1998
New edition first published 1999
This edition first published 2008

1 3 5 7 9 10 8 6 4 2

Text copyright © Stephen Waller 1996
Illustrations copyright © Kay Dixey 1996

The moral right of the author and of the illustrator has been asserted

Typeset by Graphicraft Ltd, Hong Kong
Set in 12/14pt Bembo
Printed in China
SWTC/01

Published by Pearson Education Ltd in association with
Penguin Books Ltd, both companies being subsidiaries of Pearson Plc

For a complete list of the titles available in the Penguin Readers series please write to your local
Pearson Longman office or to: Penguin Readers Marketing Department, Pearson Education,
Edinburgh Gate, Harlow, Essex CM20 2JE, England.